It Started in Waycross

M'Alan B

It Started in Waycross

Published by BooxAi

ISBN: 978-965-578-762-7

It Started in Waycross

M'Alan B

CONTENTS

Introduction

A tale of youth in the rural south. Young kids in the early 80's, teens in the late 80's to young Kings in the 90's. A journey of humble beginnings, adversity, success, and the value of 'mentorship.'

MAIN CHARACTERS

KHALIL -the main character (his journey to manhood with his cousins)

ANTON -the young mentor and co-star of the story (an extraordinary adolescent destined)

NOLAN -Khalil's first cousin on Khalil's mom's side (his sister is Layla)

NILES -another first cousin on Khalil's mom's side of the family

PAYNE WATTERS -antagonist, a menace and bully.

DERRICK BLACKHEAD -Payne's protege

LAMARCUS AND ORION WATTERS -Payne's younger brothers, special athletes on the gridiron and bullies also.

SHANNON -an alcoholic flunky of Payne.

SEBASTIAN -Khalil's grandfather on his dad's side. Anton's main mentor and silent partner to those kids.

ELLIS - Khalil's grandfather on his mother's side. (Genna is his wife)

MONIFAH -Khalil's older sister

AUNT LINDA -Nolan's mother

KHALAN - Khalil's youngest uncle on his mother's side.

CHRIS -Khalil's youngest uncle, is on his dad's side.

VANCE -Khalil's much older cousin on his mom's side (via Petersburg, FL)

RELLA -Khalil's cousin on his dad's side (Uncle Roy's daughter)

UNCLE ROY -Khalil's uncle on his dad's side (a DJ with all the latest technology and equipment for the times)

QUINN -Anton's grandfather

SADIE -Anton's grandmother

KAM -Anton's father

HENRIETTA -Anton's secret lover

BELINDA -a voluptuous teenager, a summer visitor from Florida (with 304 tendencies)

REESHA -Nolan's first baby mother

ROCHELLE -young, curvy, promiscuous local

MR. NELSON -a major player moving forward in this trilogy.

Chapter One

THE YOUNG MENTOR ANTON

Anton didn't know all the details, but he did know that his mother was in jail with a life sentence. She loved his dad too hard and shot him because she wasn't going to share him with other women. She was a beautiful Hispanic woman who went off the rails.

Anton's father Kam learned some key Spanish phrases; he learned enough to greet her and to ask her to teach him more. That's how he made his breakthrough with her. Her English was choppy, and her family was one of the very few Hispanic families in Waycross at the time.

Anton was raised bilingual as a result during his early childhood before the tragedy of his father. After the devastating scenario, his mother's family moved back to Brazil, and his grandparents lovingly took him in. His deceased father's parents. They adored their only grandchild. Anton loved his mom dearly, but it was hard to like her because she killed his hero.

For the next few years, Anton absorbed information like a computer, always around the grand folks watching, listening, and learning. Otherwise, he was basically an introvert. The only kid he was consistent with was Khalil. For some reason, he naturally took on a big brother role with his young next-door neighbor.

It was Saturday at about 11 am. Anton just finished having tea with his grandfather Quinn. Quinn was telling him that he'd be grown before he knew it, so don't rush it; enjoy your childhood; it's too short not to. Then he'd replay these 'basics' for Anton, "The only thing Sadie and I need from you is respect, clean up behind yourself, and handle your chores...for the sake of karma and goodwill, you should want to be a positive person so I don't demand that as much as you should demand it from yourself."

Anton heard this message from his grandfather (Quinn) and could deliver the words verbatim. Anton could only take the well-intended advice with a grain of salt. His own dad proved to him that life was short. His dad didn't even reach 30 before his untimely demise.

Anton's drive was actually stimulated by the advice his father offered early on. His dad told him at eight that life would only give you lemons, and you have to make the lemonade. Anton saw enough folks struggling to realize what he didn't want for himself.

He was motivated to have a lemonade stand to earn a few bucks that same day. His father was also a jui-jujitsu practitioner; Kam taught his son how important self-discipline was before he taught him the art of self-defense.

Anton only needed a fraction of a second to submit someone. An arm bar, wrist lock, chokeholds, etc. At a very young age, he was instilled with a drive to grow rich and to be able to defend himself. After enjoying his tea with his grandfather Quinn, he noticed Khalil in his front yard with his Tonka trucks and Hot Wheels.

Anton was always planning, plotting, reasoning, studying, listening. Always wanting to be better in areas of fitness, self-defense, finance, apprenticeship, and leadership. This young lad was mostly serious; it could be arduous just watching Anton's focus and determination at work.

What people didn't know was his father instilled some principles in his young son early that basically set him apart. These principles and his dad's demise seemed to be the cocktail that propelled his determination to a very high level. He was, in so many ways, a very young adult.

Anton had a great nonchalant attitude in general; however, beneath the surface was a fierce warrior spirit. Anton was equipped mentally, morally, and exceptionally so for a kid his age.

Chapter Two

ENTREPRENEURIAL SPIRITS

The late 70's, almost 1980.

Khalil was oblivious to Anton's bird's eye view of his 'roadways.' With the help of his Tonka truck, 'construction' was complete. Khalil constructed a 'scene' outside the front of his trailer home in an area of dirt that had a few clumps of grass that looked more like trees in the make-believe world young Khalil created to escape his reality. He had a very strong imagination for a kid so young. Anton was four years older than Khalil yet was still impressed by the setup, but what he really liked was how engaged Khalil was in his fantasy. Anton crossed into Khalil's 'creation.'

"Come back to earth, little Architect. I want to quiz you, see how you think."

Khalil was so engrossed with his roadways in the dirt that he was surprised by Anton's voice.

"Oh, ok," was Khalil's response as he got up off his knees to address his older neighbor.

After Khalil got up and dusted off his knees, he asked, "What's an architect?"

"Good question because I misused the word...an architect deals with buildings, and you didn't make buildings; you have roadways; I guess you're a civil engineer."

Khalil loved the sound of that and looked at his 'construction project' again, then smiled. He was always learning something from Anton; his interactions were always appreciated. The big brother he always wanted, it seemed.

Now older, Anton focuses his mind on making money. He has all summer to execute his ideas, and he's sure his young neighbor Khalil could learn something and be of use.

Anton definitely felt he had some great ideas, and he felt he was ready to lead young Khalil. Anton had some valuable routines. Besides his own grandfather, he had a schedule with Khalil's grandad (on his father's side), Sebastian... he learned aspects of farming and how to be diplomatic when it comes to leadership.

Anton usually met Sebastian in front of his vast garden early Saturday a.m. Anton was there to help Sebastian do whatever he needed, from plowing to watching Sebastian wring chicken necks, and then Anton would begin the process of plucking the feathers and draining the blood.

Summer is about to begin, and Anton has some ideas to get money. He cuts up loose leaf paper into the size of business cards then he goes to speak to his possible business associate Khalil.

"We have all summer to get money; if you want to get money with me, you have to be willing to pull your weight."

Then Anton hands him the blank cut-up paper.

"What am I supposed to do with all this cut-up paper?"

"Write down the services we are providing, what we do. Take your time and write it nice and neat, here use this pen after you practice. If it's done correct, I can put my house phone number at the bottom. This evening I'll put our business 'cards' on all our closest neighbors' doors."

Khalil liked the idea. He took the cut-up paper inside his humble dwelling and went to work on a business card. He sat at the kitchen table and began to think about what the card should say. He thought about the things Anton could do and the things he could do himself.

On a scrap piece of paper, he practiced writing and sat there wondering what to write. Finally, he was satisfied with what he had: lawn service, running errands for the elderly, and Sebastian's fresh roasted peanuts for sale.

The front of the card simply said Ankhal Services. Khalil wasn't that well versed yet at his young age, but he was coming along well. His very strict but well-spoken mother helped him with the diction by translating what he originally wrote for the back of the card. At 7 years old, he wasn't using terms like 'specializing.'

His mother didn't let him go out much, but one of the few people outside of the Kingdom Hall she let Khalil associate with was Anton. Khalil's mother tried to 'witness' to Anton about her religion one day, and Anton politely declined, then added,

"I love God, ma'am, I talk and pray to him every day. Khalil is my little bro, I can tell he loves God too, if he didn't, I wouldn't have a little bro."

Khalil's mother's initial respect for Anton increased twofold after that interaction. In her mind, Anton was her son's big brother. Most times, when Khalil's mother had something to do, she only had to take Khalil's older sister Monifah with her.

That summer was to be the beginning of understanding what good ideas, partnership, and hard work could produce.

A few hours later, Anton saw young Khalil pushing his family's bright red lawnmower in neat lines around the cheap trailer home they lived in. Khalil was out in the wicked hot sun getting the job done.

He was finishing up, but not looking closely enough, Khalil mowed over an ant hill, FIRE ANTS! In mere moments, those ants were all over Khalil, getting past his shoes and socks to defend their mound and Queen.

Khalil shrieked in pain as those ants made their presence felt, stinging him in mass as he left the lawnmower to run from his mistake. While Khalil was tending to his stings, Anton finished up the lawn for him then waited on the front steps to see what the cards looked like.

Khalil came back out five minutes later after putting some ointment on. Anton could tell Khalil was still disturbed by what just happened.

"You know that anthill was there first. It didn't jump in your way in the last minute, and in this Georgia heat, the best time to cut grass is in the early morning, or near sundown. Before you start cutting your grass you're suppose to walk around the yard and pick up anything you don't want your mower running over and navigate around anything like anthills...now let me see one of our business cards."

(Anton thought 7 was a bit young for his mother to have him out there cutting grass, but if Khalil followed his advice, he'd be fine with the chore from now on, especially since that's what they'd be doing for the bulk of their income to start).

Anton was impressed with the front of the card, in all caps, he liked it: ANKHAL SERVICES. He smiled when he read the back.

"Did your mother help you with this?"

"Uh huh, she suggested the word 'services' instead of me writing 'stuff,' and she taught me the word 'specialize.'"

"I'm about to go home and write my phone number on these cards so we can set our business in motion, you did good."

It was the first time Khalil actually used a pen, at his current age, he was using pencils. That summer was exciting and new to this young business duo. Anton wrote his phone number on all 100 of their cards. The first stop was to drop off 20 cards to Khalil. Then Anton passed out 50 cards to the closest prospective neighbors.

Anton knew half the folks in the area preferred to do their own yard work, but if their prices were the best and the work was up to par, they'd end up with more than enough clientele.

After Anton came back from his 'business trip,' he found Khalil making roadways in the dirt again. It was time to talk business, though.

"Do you think your sister wants to be a part of our business?"

"My sister doesn't do yard work."

"We are not limiting ourselves to yard work, lil bro; let me explain my vision to you. First off, we have to have clientele. My grandad has something called an edger that lines up the perimeter of the yard. It was left to him by my great-uncle. If I use it right, it'll be the difference between us and anyone else trying to do what we're doing."

Anton let Khalil digest his words for a moment, then continued, "The fact that we'll probably be the youngest and the most gracious, we should at least get the opportunity to gain customers; our performance is what keeps them. I even have a diagonal style to cut the grass that I plan to use as a trademark that it's our work to make us unique. Combine that with the edging and the clean-up that should set us apart."

Anton then went on to continue to recruit Khalil's sister for the near future.

"If your sister wants in, she'll be helping us stay organized, and she'll be running our Lemonade/Fruit stand in the shade, of course. We just need her to make some business cards for us. Tell her to make as many as she can, and it should say something like this:

"1019 Blackwell St. Sweet fruit baskets Lemonade or something like that."

Anton paused before rambling his vision, "When we start getting paid from the yard work, we'll be able to invest in our fruit stand; down the line, I envision us possibly getting a food cart...that's when we'll have conversations with our grandmothers, the best cooks in the world... I like the name you came up with for our business; you combined our names An(ton)Khal(lil) Services...I'll be up early with the edger to show you how I line up the yard like a fine barber."

Chapter Three

ANKHAL SERVICES

A month after writing the business name and services on makeshift cards, the duo had more than enough clientele. Monifah was in her second week of selling lemonade and fruit baskets in front of the trailer. She was never by herself.

Monifah was highly capable, smart and efficient, but quiet and shy. Monifah let her cousin Cynthia, one of Sebastian's many granddaughters, deal with the customers for the most part. They were about the same age and Cynthia was a social butterfly. She would only be available for the next two summers. Cynthia would be back living in Atlanta with her mother after that.

THE SETUP ANKHAL SERVICES PROVIDED WAS effective. A short table that was long and wide. They spotted the table thrown out as garbage, possibly because one of the short, thick legs was broken on it. Anton told Sebastian about the table. Sebastian agreed to drive them in his pickup to inspect for possible repairs, to assess if it was worth the effort. Sebastian ultimately came through for them as usual. With a portion of the profits from landscaping, they invested in their fruit stand.

THE FRUIT WAS MOSTLY FROM SEBASTIAN'S GARDEN (watermelon and cantaloupe) his plum and peach trees. Khalil's grandad Sebastian was a silent partner, and very instrumental. He had small business knowledge and was aware of loopholes and benefits that could be taken advantage of legally. He learned a lot about this earlier when he was getting doors closed in his face. Sebastian would certainly support Anton because he saw the promise and potential in the bright, focused youths, and wanted to help them flex their wings.

Sebastian made sure he had fresh roasted peanuts available to sell at their fruit stand. Khalil thought to name the fruit stand THE OASIS, Anton agreed. They invested in some very large coolers and set Monifah up every day by noon. During the hot summer, she was strategically placed in the shade of the pecan tree in front of their modest dwelling, with Cynthia taking the lead.

One morning, when Khalil woke up, he realized that his bike had been stolen...he usually brought it into the trailer to avoid that misfortune, but he somehow forgot that time.

A day later, he saw this bully named Derrick Blackhead riding a bike that looked just like his. It was just sloppily spray-painted black. Khalil instantly took it as a loss and a lesson.

He'd never confront Derrick; Khalil was more of a track star than a fighter anyway. He definitely wasn't like Anton in that regard. In fact, Khalil thought about how Anton handled conflict and wished he had the heart and skill to handle bullies.

One day, the most menacing bully picked the wrong one…The Watters were an infamous trio of brothers. They never were together too much except when the younger two went to elementary school. The younger two brothers were of no concern to Anton (they could be Khalil's concern, though).

The oldest, named Payne, was the original 'Deebo,' bike included. He was much bigger and a year older than Anton. It seemed Payne was always working on his legs. He had a big 18-speed bike that he kept on the hardest gears (settings). Payne's sturdy, powerful, long legs would allow him to glide smoothly over all terrain, and Waycross had a lot of dirt roads at the time.

One day, Payne got off his bike and walked up to Anton to explain his 'protection fees'…Anton told him his services weren't needed because God was his protection.

Payne smiled at him mischievously, then put his entire frame into a body shot that made Anton wince, then wheeze and doubled over in extreme pain. Payne then told Anton that his fees were only $20 a week to continue to do business on his block.

As Payne talked, Anton recovered and stood straight up, defiant, eyes ablaze and focused. He told Payne that his body shot was free of charge and that if he left him alone, all would be forgiven and then forgotten. Payne laughed, then went to throw another body shot. Anton was ready this time. As Payne threw the punch, Anton sidestepped it and then quickly looped Payne's arm for a devastating armbar resulting in intense pain and torn ligaments in Payne's arm.

Payne's father paid Anton a visit after his eldest son came back from the hospital in a sling. After a brief conversation, they shook hands. Mr. Watters was impressed with the young lad and wanted him to teach his younger sons how to fight. Anton told him that he'd never trained anyone and he'd never train bullies.

Chapter Four

GROWN DECISIONS AT A YOUNG AGE

Khalil's parents had a very tumultuous relationship, very rocky. They tried and failed numerous times to have a healthy relationship. The very last time they tried resulted in Khalil's younger brother being conceived.

Khalil was 8 now and progressing nicely, but at the end of the day he was still merely a child, and as a child he shouldn't have to make adult decisions about which parent to live with. Unfortunately, that's what his mother asked him. His parents got into a skirmish that resulted in his father being cut in his hand by his mother who was holding the scissors.

In his heart he knew he didn't want to continue to live the JW (Jehovah's Witness) lifestyle with his mother, but he didn't want to hurt his mom's feelings. When his mother posed the horrible question, he thought about his big bro and business partner Anton. Khalil just wanted to continue on with his big bro. The easiest way to do that was to live under his grandfather Sebastian's roof.

Bottomline Khalil was tired of being a 'special' Jehovah's Witness because he actually felt like an oddball, far from special, and that so-called 'pioneer work' was embarrassing to him, going door to door in a cheap 2 piece suit quoting his favorite Bible verse :

Revelation 21:4, 'He will wipe every tear from their eyes. There will be no more death or mourning or crying or pain, for the old order of things has passed away."

THE SAME DAY HIS MOTHER ASKED HIM TO CHOOSE, young Khalil moved into the house behind his trailer. Now he resided at his grandparents' (Sebastian) house on his dad's side of the family.

In the following months, Khalil's mother witnessed (pioneer work) to an older lady whose nephew stayed with her. He was divorced from his wife of many years and was a great help to his aunt.

The man was drawn to Khalil's mother in such a way that he accepted everything that Khalil didn't religiously. He started having Bible study with her and it seemed he accepted a religion he wasn't totally into just to be with Khalil's mother. The man came through like a hero too as he courted her well. In the midst of courting her, he paid an exterminator-type visit and won the war against the roaches when he fumigated her trailer home.

Soon after he married her, they relocated to Richmond, VA, for better economic opportunities. Khalil was going to miss his sister, but not his crybaby little brother. Khalil's mother was using reusable cloth diapers that his sister and he had to deal with after his mother changed him.

KHALIL WAS NEVER RAISED BY HIS DAD AFTER ALL. After a few weeks of being around, his dad relocated to Albany, then moved again, starting a new family. It seemed like his dad's first family was practiced because his next marriage lasted till death did them apart.

Chapter Five

COUSIN NOLAN

Nolan was an adventurous, high-spirited kid. He maintained a great demeanor regardless of having a father addicted to heroin. His father's addiction made things very hard for that family.

Nolan wasn't in Waycross at this time. Of the three cousins (Khalil, Nolan, and Niles, all from Grandad Ellis), he was the only one who lived in Florida/Ft. Lauderdale. His early years before arriving in Waycross were filled with constant moving caused mostly by evictions, witnessing his mom get bullied for her check, and being physically abused because Nolan's father had to have his high by any means necessary.

Always changing schools, never had decent school clothes, and the only motivation to go to school was the free lunch. Sometimes, their mother wouldn't even allow them to go to school because their garments were too shabby.

Through it all, the surprising part was Nolan's disposition. Despite his circumstances, his mind was bright, and he was very observant, traits that helped him navigate his early challenges.

Nolan's mom had enough of the abuse, evictions, and all the rest that comes with having a dopefiend husband.

To be clear, both of Khalil's parents came from very big families. He has a great number of aunts and uncles on both sides. In fact, on his mother's side of the family, Granddaddy Ellis and his wife purposely had a lot of children specifically to be field hands. It was a solution for survival back in those times.

Of all the cousins that came from his aunts and uncles on his mom's side, Khalil built strong bonds with Nolan and then Niles.

The situation Nolan had in Florida reached an apex. The family arrived to the rescue. Led by Grandaddy Ellis, the family came four deep to bring them back to Waycross. They all stuffed themselves in a sedan and made the crowded trip back to Waycross.

Initially, they stayed with their grandparents until they were able to get an apartment on Gilmore Street not too long after being in Waycross. They lived around the most blatantly racist white folks, the poor ones. The kids of racist white folks were slow to adopt the racist attitude of their parents, so Nolan and his younger sister Layla had lots of fun playing with the white kids until they were able to move into a rented trailer right down the street from their grandparents on Wadley Street.

CHAPTER SIX

FIRST COUSINS FINALLY MEET

Nolan actually didn't run into his cousin Khalil until almost a year after being in Waycross. Since Khalil now lived on his dad's side of the family, he wasn't in an organic position to meet a cousin he didn't even know from his mother's side of the family.

Khalil was an astute student of his big brother's business partner Anton, so he thought to make it a routine to go visit his granddad Ellis on his mother's side of the family. Khalil casually mentioned the idea to Anton. Not only did Anton think it was a good idea, he offered to go with him. Anton always appreciated opportunities to be around the elders; he always felt that if you listen to them, they will give you 'jewels' that are keys to life. This is the main reason why he has routines with his own grandfather, Quinn, and Khalil's grandfather, Sebastian.

So one Sunday, Anton and Khalil rode their shiny brand new bikes (business was indeed good) over to Khalil's grandparents' house... The first person Khalil noticed was Nolan sitting on the screened-in porch in a rocking chair. His granddad had a job for him that a.m.

Khalil spoke to Nolan through the screen door.

"Hey Blood, I came to see grandad, what's your name?"

"I'm Nolan, I'm just waiting for grandad to come out, he has some work for me to do this morning." (young Nolan was impressed with the bikes and gear they wore, then imagined how pathetic he probably looked to them).

"I'm your Aunt Linda's son, you must be Aunt Anne's son, I saw your sister, she left like last week though."

Khalil's marveled at his intuition (then he thought about his sister). He then recovered to confirm his identity and then he introduced his business partner Anton to him as well.

Khalil noticed how tattered Nolan's garments were, then just chalked it up to him dressing for some grimy, challenging work grandad Ellis had for him. Fundamentally Khalil assumed correctly, but at that time he didn't realize that Nolan's wardrobe didn't get too much better than that, regardless of what he was doing.

Nolan was impressed and envious of his cousins' look of success combined with his height (Khalil was tall for his age, taller than the older Nolan).

Khalil and Nolan made small talk and learned a bit about each other's lives in a short time while Anton simply listened in. Not long after, their steady and highly principled grandfather came out to start his day.

"Oh, you have some helpers, Nolan...you finally ran into your cousin?"

"No sir, they don't look dressed for the job, they just came to visit you grandad."

Anton spoke up, "Good day sir, I'm Khalil's business partner, Anton" (he proceeded to close the distance, then firmly shook Khalil's grandfather's hand).

"These types of visits can be enriching, so I decided to tag along so I wouldn't miss out on an opportunity to learn something."

"Business partners?!!... What business?"

At that point, Anton presented grandfather Ellis with two business cards (they had real ones now, not those makeshift pieces of paper in writing). Ellis took his reading glasses out of his shirt pocket to read the cards:

"Ankhal Services... You young fellas do all this?" Young professionals, I see... y'all off to a good start... if I didn't have Nolan here, I probably would've hired y'all. Nolan gets distracted, but he works hard, maybe y'all could fit him in y'all's business."

Khalil thought it was a great idea, but that was Anton's department. Khalil's job in the business was to be creative and follow Anton's lead.

The job that grandad Ellis had for Nolan was especially for a fearless type like him. He was to go under the house and remove all debris...Khalil would never, and Anton could think of a myriad of other ways to get money that wouldn't have you potentially blindsided by snakes and rodents.

Anton was a bit impressed by Nolan's willingness to do such a job. Anton told Nolan to come over to Blackwell

Street later to talk business if he wanted to be a part of their hustle. Khalil told him they'd be in front of Uncle Khalan's trailer 1019. Nolan saw his uncle a few times at his grandad's when he got to Waycross, now he was finally going to see where he lived.

Chapter Seven

BIG BUSINESS

In the summer Anton and Khalil would only take Sundays off from business during the summer. No landscaping, errands, etc., scheduled at all; only the fruit stand stayed open all summer from noon till 8 and since Monifah was gone, Sebastian decided to sit with his granddaughter Cynthia to keep that portion of the business going smoothly.

It was the last month of summer and Anton was sharing more ideas about expanding the business and possibly hiring Khalil's cousin Nolan while they stood around The Oasis (the name of the fruit stand).

"Our summer hustle will be over soon, but we can get money all year round if we get a food cart... and if we commit to your cousin Nolan, he's a partner not an employee… we don't have employees, we have partners… this ain't employment, we profit share with business partners… but if profit was a pie, we definitely have earned the biggest slices so far."

Khalil was hoping Nolan got the opportunity, so he asked, "How will you know if he should be a partner?"

"I'll have a good idea after I see how he reacts to these 10 commandments I've adopted from some good reading… I tested you differently, I simply gave you cut-up paper to see if you could make our business cards and you actually came up with the name of our business, Ankhal Services, our fruit stand, The Oasis, we are equally dedicated and I'm sure you'll just continue to be 'innovative,' look that word up he grinned."

"No need to, according to the context clues it means creative."

Anton nodded. They gave each other that Ankhal dap.

They must've talked Nolan up, because he was walking up to them in some different garments from earlier… less tattered, but still he dressed homely. Regardless of his dress, Khalil was happy to see his blood, it was something about Nolan that Khalil gravitated to. He had a sincerity about him and was fearless in aspects Khalil couldn't relate to. Anton saw him and just wanted him to be successful in his 'interview' for a partnership. If he was, they would immediately upgrade his wardrobe and give him his older bike. A business expense to be paid back in reasonable increments, Anton thought. He had to pass the test, though, bottom line.

They all welcomed Nolan as if he was dressed sharply in a three-piece suit; even Cynthia managed not to turn up her nose at Khalil's bummy cousin; her expression was neutral and businesslike.

Anton then proceeded to lead the cousins away from The Oasis to the picnic table by the fruit trees on the side of Sebastian's house. Anton told them both to take a seat at the picnic table. After they were seated, Anton began and kept it very simple... "Your partnership will be based on how you respond to our business principles...we have Ankhal Service's 10 Commandments, all adopted from a good book I read. You must agree to follow them, but how you feel about the commandments is just as important, you understand so far?"

"I understand what you said, but if I'm going to follow the commandments, why does it matter how I feel about them?"

Anton liked the question, then responded:

"If you agree with the words the commandments are easier to follow, that's why."

Khalil remained silent as he was in awe of his witty business partner and mentor, thinking to himself how was he even a partner because he didn't even know the 10 commandments.

Simultaneously, Nolan quickly became unsure also, then minimized himself and responded, "I'm not religious, I'm not into commandments. I just respect people...just hire me to do anything y'all don't feel like doing... I'll do anything to get fresh like y'all."

Anton studied him for a moment, then said, "We would hire desperate immigrants before we hired one of our Kings in disguise...Ankhal Services ain't here to feel sorry for you. Fortunately, we're in a better position, we can actually help you tap into your skillset and learn about business early. They are not teaching this game in elementary school or high school! Are you ready to digest these commandments, youngin?"

Nolan humbly took in all that was said and then replied, "I'm ready to hear the commandments," he almost sighed.

Anton handed Khalil a folded piece of paper from out of his back pocket, then instructed him to read the commandments and for Nolan to respond to each one:

1. NEVER SHAKE A MAN'S HAND WHILE SITTING down.

"I agree with that."

2. IN A NEGOTIATION, NEVER MAKE THE FIRST offer.

"I can do that, but I don't understand; if I know what I want, why can't I just say it?"

KHALIL ANSWERED HIM AS ANTON FIGURED HE would. "You may know what you want, but what you don't know is how much the other person is willing to pay...they may have been willing to offer more than you wanted, then you've just lowballed yourself." Anton was loving this, and continued to pay close attention to the interaction.

3. When shaking hands, grip firmly and look them in the eye.

"I agree, no shady handshakes."

4. Don't let a wishbone grow where a backbone should be.

"I agree; I'm here to make things happen with y'all not wishing upon a star."

5. Be like a duck. Remain calm on the surface and paddle like crazy underneath.

"I agree." Anton finally interjected, he said "Always control your emotions; it's called composure."

Khalil continued...

6. Give credit, take blame.

"I will be polite and responsible."

7. Be confident and humble at the same time.

"I agree."

8. In all things, lead by example, not explanation.

"I agree."

9. Stand up to bullies.

"I agree." Anton studied Khalil's face after that one, then told Khalil to repeat the commandment... Khalil repeated it, and Anton told them that they would be addressing that topic again, "We are the only means of security for our business; we have to be able to protect it."

10. Manners make the man.

"I agree."

Anton took the dialogue back over.

"There are 3 bonus commandments too

1. Write down your dreams

2. Write your own eulogy... never stop revising it.

3. Lastly, never turn down a breath mint."

Both cousins laughed at that last one; Khalil then taught Nolan 'the greeting' an Ankhal Services thing.

Anton pulled Khalil to the side and told Khalil that he was going to their safe (Sebastian made this possible). They kept secure in a back corner of the shed to get the money for the shopping trip.

When Anton found out Nolan had a sister just a year

younger than him, he told Nolan that he was representing his family and that if he wanted his sister in the business she could be in on his strength of him. Nolan got extremely excited, he felt his life was taking a turn for the better.

Anton doubled back to the safe to grab an extra $50 (giving Khalil a total of $150 with instructions to keep all receipts for business/tax reasons). Nolan's sister Layla could 'get fresh' too.

Anton admitted to Khalil that the investment in Nolan is a risk...and even though it's calculated it still could back-fire...as a business, Anton admits this was more of a humanitarian decision than a business decision. Nolan didn't disappoint, though. It took about 10 weeks to repay the advance, so everything worked out.

Sebastian was the only one in the front seat. Anton would've sat in the front with him, but he didn't come; he had other affairs in mind. Nolan loved riding in the bed of the truck. Khalil didn't mind in this case because Nolan's energy made it cool, but it's not his preference.

They first went to pick up Layla, and she was happily in disbelief when she found herself in the front seat of the truck with Sebastian on her way to shop. There was no K-Mart on this trip; they were going to the mall. Nolan also got a bonus surprise when Khalil told him that Anton said he could use his old bike that was secure in his grandparent's backyard. This was one of the best days of Nolan's early life.

Nolan and Layla appreciated their new clothes. Confident but humble was the commandment he remembered as he tried on his new tennis shoes. Layla couldn't stop smiling as she tried on her capris and fitted top. They both had enough new clothes to cover almost a week. They never had so many nice things. Their mother was explained everything by Sebastian when he dropped Layla off from shopping. Nolan was going to ride back with Sebastian and Khalil so he could get the bicycle that was promised to him. Their mother responded sarcastically towards Nolan,

"You're good for something after all, huh?!" Then she went back to her beer and television.

Chapter Eight

TRANSITIONS

Khalil and Nolan were entering adolescence, both around 12 years old and going on 20. Time flies when you're young, busy and successful.

Khalil's mother left her property on 1019 Blackwell Street to her youngest brother, Khalan, to rent. The old trailer was removed, and now a nice double-wide trailer occupied 1019 Blackwell Street.

The first thing Anton thought to do was secure the space under the pecan tree to continue to have The Oasis at the same familiar and convenient location. For what was probably a weekend 'Malt Liquor Fee' of $10 a week, Khalil's Uncle Khalan agreed to let them continue to use that space.

Anton also made a deal with Khalan that also allowed Nolan to stay in the trailer. Now Layla has her own room in the rented trailer with her mom on Wadley Street.

Khalil would miss his sister the most. It's not like they got along perfectly; in fact, no one could perturb him more at times. This was before Anton became a daily influence that helped him to see the big picture. Khalil used to let his older sister's mocking set him into temper tantrums that made him seem like a young hothead. All that changed once Khalil asked her if she wanted to be a part of their business.

They really had a true appreciation for each other before she left with the rest of his family to Virginia. He didn't keep up with his mom and the rest of them, mostly because of the religion. That's why he didn't call or write them. Out of sight, out of mind, it was for Khalil. He started wondering how his sister was doing after Nolan mentioned her coming down from Virginia for part of the summer. Khalil thought about how cool it would be if she came back down to stay for good. He was staying with his dad's parents, and he thought she could stay with their mother's parents like she did the past summer.

CHAPTER NINE

COUSIN NILES JOINS THE FREY

Nolan had never met his cousin, Niles. This was the first introduction. However, Khalil remembered the first encounter they had about five or six years ago:

Khalil remembered when Niles got dropped off at his dwelling, but not as well as Niles did. For Niles, it was a break from an otherwise traumatic childhood. Fond moments were built between Khalil and Niles. Khalil and Monifah were so nice to him. Khalil taught him how to ride a bike and brought him out of his silence with all the high-energy childhood games they could muster.

Khalil didn't know why Niles was mute initially when they met. All Khalil knew was he had someone to play with who just seemed different until he got comfortable and started speaking. Then he just seemed like a regular cool kid.

Niles, unfortunately, had experienced some toxic moments in his young life.

His parents were high school sweethearts who got married. His dad went into the military, so instead of Niles being born in Waycross, he was born at Ft. Hood, where his dad was stationed.

His mom proved to be 'for the streets,' moving in an adulterous manner powered by a newfound drug addiction in Texas. She landed back in Waycross and divorced with young Niles to raise (and that monkey on her back).

Niles's mother continued her promiscuous activities back in Waycross with no regard for Niles' innocence: Sofas were usually close to the wall... but not in this case... this sofa was a partition wall with the added distraction of a battery-powered truck that seemed to go over all terrain he created between the wall and sofa (his play area)...as he recalled it, this was his safe haven, unbothered as he recalled hearing his mother's body get penetrated aggressively.

What type of individual would this environment create? This may be how some of our monsters have been created, these toxic circumstances.

His mother always seemed to cheat on whoever the current boyfriend was. Niles was a victim of her latest boyfriend, the last one before his father (Khalil's uncle) took over his upbringing.

That last man Nile recalled didn't take too kindly to that type of disloyalty: His mother experienced a blow so powerful that it broke her thumb when she raised her hand in an attempt to deflect his fist. Domestic abuse that couldn't be justified, but a viable emotional excuse: SHE

CHEATED. He thought he owned her core, so when he put all his emotions into the blow, her thumb got cracked when she tried to protect her face as his powerful fist still landed at his intended target. Her then bruised jaw.

Niles's mother made a frantic move after that episode of abuse. She bundled Niles up with a few things and took him to the Greyhound bus stop and told him not to move, to stay seated right there until his dad came to pick him up. Just left him there. ALONE. The traumatized boy was rooted there despite needing to relieve himself in the restroom.

Strangers most likely tried to be friendly until they smelled his stench because of him not being able to tap into any common sense. His age and the distressing experience weighed heavily as he sat there spoiled. He actually bit the man's leg that attacked his mother. His reward: knocked upside the head and relegated helpless.

It's a long list of misfortune for Niles, too many to detail. In another unfortunate circumstance, he even found himself as a young boy sharing a jail cell with his mother. His dad finally got him from the bus stop that faithful day when his mom abandoned him there. After his short stay at 1019 Blackwell Street with Khalil and other relatives/friends his dad left him at, he went to Germany with his dad's new family. The Sergeant got stationed there again.

Niles mom gave him his first 6 years of trauma. His father basically oversaw the next 6 years of it.

Back from Germany, his father's next duty station was in Cali (Ft. Ord). Two years there, Niles earned his gang affiliations. Another very young CRIP. Hardened by traumatic circumstances, yet only 12 years old. The young Gangsta Niles is back in Waycross.

He pulls up to 1019 Blackwell St. with his dad. Forever the outcast, the bulk of his immediate family (his stepmother and two half-sisters) was at his grandparents' house on Wadley Street. They would stay there until it was time for Niles' dad to deploy again.

Khalil recognized Niles before he even got out of the car (the years only changed his size).

Speaking to Nolan, Khalil made his request,

"Cuz, introduce yourself to our cousin Niles, he may already remember you from that Florida visit you told me about, I need to talk to Anton."

Anton makes eye contact with Khalil and they walk off to the side.

"Anton, check and see what's going with my two uncles in that trailer."

"Why should we mind their business?"

"It might be our business?"

"How?"

"Niles got luggage, he might stay here. He'd have to share the room with Nolan if I'm right."

"Say no more young grasshopper, let's see if we can save our business about $20 extra a month. I'll be back."

Khalil walks back toward The Oasis while Anton walks toward the trailer to get informed. Inside the trailer, Khalan grins as he offers young Anton a beer,

"You're at least sixteen now, I had my first beer when I was fifteen."

As usual, Anton cooly declined, then introduced himself to Niles' father, shaking his hand.

'I'm Anton, business partner with your nephews out

there. If your son is going to be around for a bit, then he'll probably want to be a part of our business."

"You talking about that little stand outside?"

Khalan interrupted,

"Nah bro, these youngsters is out here getting it, they work hard too! Show him your business card Anton.'

After looking at the business card Niles' dad was impressed and hopeful. He knew his son felt like an outcast because of his current wife's favoritism to his daughters who came from her womb. He knew he hadn't been the best father no matter how well-intended he was. He wanted to drop Niles off in Waycross and just hope for the best. Now, he saw a great circumstance for his son. He had been taken out of his thought process by Anton.

"Do you think your son can take instruction, and be a part of a team? You're his only reference."

Young Anton was all business with this grown man, a Sergeant in the Army. The sinewy Sergeant responded,

"Niles has the potential to be good, but he's mostly a knucklehead... I don't know what to do with him some-times... He does have some nice sketches though. I wanted him to learn some discipline so I could teach him how to box. He don't listen!'

"I appreciate your reference. It's not a great one, but we'll see what we can do. I'm sure his cousins will want him onboard. Only thing left to talk about now is the deduction on the room Ankhal Services will only be paying for half a room now. That $80 monthly should now be $60.

Khalan nodded acceptance and at that moment Anton nodded at them both, then walked out.

Khalan barked, "That young mofo been here before... young bucks ain't coming out this damn slick... that kid is ALL BUSINESS!!" The Sergeant just smirked before he returned his attention to his beer. The brothers watched Anton walk out in quiet awe after Khalan's remark.

Chapter Ten

GROWTH

(It's late May 1985)

SUCCESS. IT WAS INEVITABLE... IN BUSINESS HE was a leader, bright, focused, earnest, idealistic, hardworking, highly principled, and very determined... Anton was DIFFERENT.

Their biggest stream of revenue was the landscaping in the summer. The Oasis did very well all year round on the weekends. The profit margin could be very good for the food cart because they grow all their own food. Sebastian's youngest son (of many) Chris, caught most of the fish they prepared and they got most of the chicken from Sebastian and his farmer friends at a very good price.

They would also benefit from catering certain events.

Birthdays, tailgating parties, etc. The ability to make deliveries would also provide sales for Ankhal Services (they even delivered watermelon).

The consistency and quality work of Ankhal Services provided them with strong streams of revenue. They had a nice budget to start the quest for a reasonably priced pickup truck and a good deal on a food cart. $4000 and counting for business improvements for progress.

Vance came just in time to help Ankhal Services as a partner. He was the oldest son of Khalil's mom's oldest brother...he came up from St. Petersburg, FL. His mechanic skills and ability to operate almost any vehicle were very helpful.

Initially, he just wanted to get away from his dad. Khalil's oldest uncle on his mom's side accused his son of being a freeloading bum with fantasies. Vance did have great potential to disappoint his dad. However, after running into his young cousins Khalil and Anton on a random visit to his precious Yamaha, he knew that their business could possibly need his mechanical expertise.

He'd be too far away from his dad to be accused of freeloading, he thought. Vance would sleep on Khalan's sofa in the living room until he figured out where he'd move. They'd work something out. Vance was a lady's man anyway, so he was only on Khalan's sofa rarely.

The timing was great a few weeks later when he came to stay. His partnership with Ankhal Services was actually a meeting between Anton, Chris, and Vance. Khalil was almost a fan of his older cousin Vance.

In even younger days, Vance had another bike at the time, nothing fancy; he took turns giving Khalil and his sister rides on it whenever they saw him out in the deep country. It was the deep country where all the big snakes and the crops Grandad Ellis oversaw back when he sharecropped there.

You name it, from sugarcane to tobacco, with an abundance of fruits and vegetables in between. Everything from the pig styes to the chicken pens, cows too. Khalil, Nolan, and Niles's parents were raised at that house on the farm. After raising a brood of field hands into adulthood, Grandad Ellis moved into town (Waycross) in a house on Wadley Street with his wife Genna.

Vance wasn't much into landscaping, but his technician skills were most necessary anyway. He kept Sebastian's truck and the landscaping equipment running well. He also enjoyed making deliveries (had a knack for receiving great tips). He always made punctual deliveries even though he was a major flirt with the ladies, and a conversationalist overall.

Vance joined with great timing, especially with Sebastian's recent decline in health.

Sebastian went over the logistics as he coughed and wheezed, the irony of a silent partner; Khalil's beloved grandad Sebastian was not doing well. Father Time was waging his war against him. Regardless, he was helping Ankhal Services more than ever with his knowledge about tax write-offs, keeping up the permits for the food carts/etc. If ever purchased and other business expenses, just some good ways to navigate.

Good ole Sebastian almost choked up after going over some finer points of business, then switched up and started telling them how proud of them he was of their early success...he lamented,

"In my time, I learned what I needed to learn so I could be prosperous, how to run a business, how to farm, and other little things, but in this rural racist Confederate south, they would close doors, steal your ideas, and just relegate you to an employee if they could. Your grandad (Ellis) was a sharecropper Khalil, and I ended up being an employee of my own ideas instead of owning my ideas."

He frowned at his own statement, coughed into his handkerchief, and then added,

"Y'all are starting very early, y'all smart, you guys are in a position to help others, especially when you start to empower more partners into your business. I was worried about my youngest Chris until you came along, Anton, he saw you out here younger than him being industrious, so he stepped his game up...Ankhal Services and Chris is definitely a match."

He smiled after he said that, then some violent wheezing followed...Father Time is a cruel one.

By this time, Sebastian's youngest son Chris, age twenty-one, around the same age as Vance, is helping Anton full time in the business, taking over for Sebastian with an expanded role because the business was growing. Chris found a deal on two old Ford trucks.

One was an old '74 Ford Bronco; the other was an even older but even sturdier '72 F-250 camper special. Buy one for $1500 or both for $2700.

No one was more excited about the purchases than Vance. He was looking forward to tinkering with the airflow and engine to improve the mpg and overall performance of the trucks. Vance even got $300 shaved off the price after he noticed some minor issues with the vehicles after his test drive and inspection of the vehicles. They acquired two reliable trucks for $2400. (The 80's)

After doing some patient searching, Anton and Khalil finally found a food cart in the budget. They responded to an ad in the paper. When they got to the seller, they noticed he had another, smaller cart also. The seller said he just received the smaller one and hadn't been able to advertise it yet. They ended up making a transaction for both.

The seller would do some maintenance and checks to ensure his part in the agreement. The following week, Chris and Vance would pick them up.

The food carts: It was a simple idea. Sebastian's wife made the best collard greens, black eye peas, macaroni and cheese, string beans, cabbage, baked fish and chicken. She stopped cooking beef and fried foods for the sake of Sebastian's health. Doctors orders.

On the flip side, Anton's grandma Sadie specialized in fried chicken and fish. Also, as a baker, she made the best cobblers and cookies. Anton and Khalil agreed to sell no red meat... after they heard about Sebastian's heart condition and his doctor's orders. It was the most expensive anyway. Anton did some light research to confirm that red meat contributed heavily to heart disease. Khalil always just thought it took too long to digest. The food carts were utilized on the weekends during school. Once summer vacation started, they were open full-time.

Anton knew they could make a killing if ribs and grilled burgers were on the food cart, too. He didn't want to do that, though, he always encouraged customers who wanted red meat available to get their own cart and make it available. It was actually good advice because folks couldn't get enough of some pork chops, steaks, ribs, hamburgers, hotdogs, etc., in Waycross.

Ankhal Services didn't sell that; it was just chicken and fish with some of the best side dishes ever. He was tempted to sell shrimp until he read a science book that compared shrimp to roaches; the book referred to them as sea roaches.

Garlington Heights proved to be the most lucrative location for the bigger food cart; the smaller cart was at The Oasis.

Sebastian's wife showed her granddaughter Rella how to prepare her signature dishes for the food truck so she could spend more time tending to Sebastian. Anton's grandmother Sadie received relief from her duties too because she taught Layla how to prepare her delectable desserts and fried foods. On Saturdays and Sundays, one food cart was stationed beside The Oasis (1019 Blackwell St) and was managed by Vance and Khalil. The other cart was managed by Anton, Chris, and Nolan. They had to be very observant and lead with caution in Garlington Heights, but it was worth the risk to be there.

The crack epidemic arrived in Waycross and starred in Garlington Heights. It made the area a very lucrative location to set up shop. Those crack dealers loved that food their cousins prepared and any other folks that could afford it. They had a rule not to accept food stamps.

Anton reasoned, "If you only have food stamps that means go to the store and buy groceries, not platters." All money wasn't acceptable, and even though he served drug dealers too, he had boundaries he referred to as 'certain principles' he stood on. Khalil went right along with those principles.

Chris had his own car, but when he realized that the local women were more receptive to him when he was driving one of the business trucks he sort of traded his own car to the business to be fair...he preferred to utilize one of the trucks, the 250. Anton would drive the car James donated to the business when he went to school and for small errands. It was a clean 1978 Ford Pinto.

Since their business called for the trucks primarily, and because Chris, Vance, and Anton were the only ones with a license to drive, Chris having the truck full time was no issue, especially since he donated his car (or traded it in) Khalil asked Anton if they should get their logo on both sides of the Pinto. Anton replied,

"After I graduate and leave for boot camp that's the first thing I want you to do partner...I'm low-key in the car till I leave for basic training...advertisements would draw unwanted attention for some moves I make." Khalil looked at his mentor curiously before getting back into focus.

Vance usually drove his Yamaha in his leisure. He even made some of the small deliveries on his bike. Because of Ankhal Services, neither Chris nor Vance would ever have to go job hunting. Chris sold fresh fish on the side and Vance did side work as a mechanic when it was convenient.

Sebastian's pickup truck ran no more. Chris was using it for fishing trips. Sebastian couldn't really drive it because of his declining health. Chris used it during the week on his fishing expeditions because he didn't want that F250 Camper smelling fishy at all. Chris was glad when they found some great deals on trailers to tow the landscaping equipment on. That meant the truck could basically stay clean.

To show a form of appreciation and respect, Vance, Anton and Khalil gutted out the old, well-used truck, and with help from Chris and Nolan, they refurbished it...The nicely painted, gutted-out truck was now a fixture at The Oasis.

They used the bed of the truck to sell robustly sweet watermelons and Sebastian's favorite snack combination. FRESH ROASTED PEANUTS AND LEMONADE. On the sides of the truck, it read: SEBASTIAN'S FRESH ROASTED PEANUTS.

Chapter Eleven

KHALIL'S SISTER

Preceding the summer of 1985, Monifah wrote a letter to 1019 Blackwell Street to Khalil. She didn't know Sebastian's address, so she mailed the letter to their old address in hopes that their Uncle Khalan would give it to Khalil (still sealed).

One Saturday afternoon, after Anton and Khalil returned from landscaping, his Uncle Khalan handed him a letter (at this point, Nolan rode with Chris to do the other half of the landscaping operation).

Khalil was surprised to receive a letter in this way, but even more surprised it was from his sister. She let him know that she was doing her best to be a faithful JW and make her mom happy. In the letter, she explained when she visited in the summer, she would basically confine herself to their grandparents on their mother's side of the family which was very easy for her. She liked to get lost in books, and she was a very avid reader, so she never saw Khalil those few summers when she visited. Things were changing, though, Monifah and her mother were not getting along too well. Some of the things about the JW organization didn't seem sound, they started to seem like a cult to her. She said she missed The Oasis, Khalil, Anton, and she wished she would've stayed back with Khalil when he decided, at eight years old, to live with Sebastian.

Anton saw Khalil's mood change like a chameleon as he read the letter. From a look of concern to a smile, a bit of dismay, then a determination set on young Khalil's face.

"You alright, partner?"

"I'm good, Ant...we need to get my sister back in the fold...when Nolan gets back with Chris from their work, I'll see if he wants to ride with me to grandad's (Ellis) house."

Chris and Nolan were just pulling up and looked a bit weary, but as soon as Khalil mentioned the 15-minute bike ride to granddad Ellis, he was reenergized and ready.

Khalil grabbed a bag of peanuts for their grandad then they headed down the street.

It was a late afternoon when Khalil and Nolan rode their bikes to their grandparents house. Khalil was going to bring up his sister. He had to find out if his grandfather would let his sister move back down to Waycross for good.

They were all on the porch, grandad Ellis in his favorite rocking chair, enjoying the peanuts they brought with Nolan and Khalil on the porch swing, letting it sway slowly as they drank lemonade.

Before he explained his sister's desire to move back, he asked his grandfather,

"Grandad, how do you think we're doing with our business and school?"

"You and Nolan are making me proud, and Layla is over here almost every evening checking on me and Sadie. She always has a story to tell when she gets off the back of Vance's bike or when Anton or Chris drops her off over here. She loves that fruit stand and cooking that good food. What do y'all call it? Oh yeah, The Oasis. I think you kids are doing well, but I don't know about your grades, how are they?"

Khalil thought to bring his report card to help make his case, and he's glad he did at that moment. Nolan was very smart, but got a bit too distracted to have top grades...he did pass his classes with a high C average though.

"Here's my report card, and Nolan has passing grades too." (Quickly side-eyeing his cousin). Ellis took his report card and put on his reading glasses. He was impressed with all those A's with a few B's sprinkled in.

Nolan then called out to their grandad,

"Grandad, how much does school grades matter when you're already involved in a business? To tell you the truth granddaddy, if it wasn't for football, I wouldn't be passing my classes, it's boring to me. I'm understanding business."

Grandad looked at him in a calm stoned face, considered him a bit, then responded,

'Son, I see how you can feel that way, but school is just another test of discipline, it ain't a hard test, especially high school. BOY I wish I could've went to school!!"

Nolan nodded in respect when grandad was finished, then grandad looked at Khalil critically. Ellis asked him if he was carrying his report card with him at all times because at that moment he knew that Khalil had a certain agenda.

"What do you want Khalil, it can't be money, because y'all have that?"

"It's about my sister, she wants to move back down here and I was wondering if she could stay with y'all and help out around the house since you have extra space. I figured that if you thought we were doing ok that she could do ok down here too. She is good for our business too. She can help Layla cook for our food carts, and help manage The Oasis."

"She doesn't want to be a Jehovah's Witness grandad."

He almost dropped his head when he said that last part, but caught himself quickly, and looked in his grandfather's eyes earnestly.

Grandad paused and studied him. This grandfather was not as jovial as Sebastian, but just as kind and thoughtful... less expressive, more stoic...

Grandad Ellis' irony was that his own daughter was slowly converting him into a JW. It was known that she was his favorite daughter. The most surprising part is he used to be a devout deacon at another church when he was share-cropping in the country it was not the same message his JW daughter spoke in Khalil's opinion...Khalil's grandad looked at him thoughtfully, seeing that he was doing quite well regardless of a religion, and agreed to look into it.

Their Grandad said he'd talk to his daughter and see what's going on with Monifah. He'd let Khalil know the decision next week after he heard from the other side of it. They sat for a while after that and talked about farming and tractors. Grandad told them some sharecropping stories from his time in the country on the farm, the harvesting, plowing, etc. Grandad Ellis looked at them thoughtfully, then cracked another peanut shell while nodding positively at his impressive grandsons.

On the way back, speeding on their bikes, Khalil asked Nolan if he thought grandad would let Monifah stay with them. Nolan was hopeful, but he simply shrugged his shoulders.

Chapter Twelve

MUSIC BUSINESS

A few days later, Khalil had another bright idea he brought to Anton.

"You know my Uncle Roy is a DJ. He has these special antennas, and some other technology stuff that gives him access to radio stations in NY. We can make cassette tapes and then sell them for at least double the amount. If we buy quality cassettes in bulk, we can get them at a discount rate. Then we can make the loudest and most clear tapes around with the best new music on it straight from New York. Depending on how much the cost of the blank cassette will determine how much profit we make, you can tell I've been paying attention to you when you say 'don't let a potential idea stay grounded in the mind and not examined for worth.'"

Anton gives Khalil a rare grin, then does the Ankhal

'official dap' greeting: Anton comes down with the pound and then Khalil does the same, what follows immediately after is the power fist, then that same fist gets tapped firmly against their own chest twice followed by the peace sign.

Then Anton said, "Let's find out how much the best quality cassettes are, then which stations in NY to tune into. Those TDK tapes are the best."

Khalil chimed in, "We'll be able to get $20 10 packs. If we sell the tapes for $7, we'll do good, and the customers will be happy... 90 minutes of the newest freshest music for $7 on a quality TDK. If we buy at least 10 packs, we would get a wholesale price of $150 for that... if the first 10 sell well, that's what we can do. Nolan and I been talking about and looking into it as soon as we started liking boom boxes."

Anton saw that his young grasshopper had done his homework and repeated the 'official dap,' then told Khalil:

"You already know what to do, let's see how we do, I think your idea is golden."

Khalil goes to tell Nolan that Anton is cool with the idea (those 2 were always talking about rap music, and Nolan was hinting his surprise purchase he was saving for, a BIG BASS BOOM BOX, and after putting away $10 a week he was a week away from his BASS BOX...

One day after cutting their Uncle Roy's lawn, they asked him about all those different antennas and wires. That's how they found out he had access to NY radio stations. Khalil told his Uncle Roy that he had an idea that would definitely get his yard cut for free. Uncle Roy just smiled and said, "I believe you, nephew," then laughed.

Later, Khalil and Nolan were discussing logistics...it

sounded like a foreign language to Niles, so he kept drawing, impressive too, all in his own world.

Khalil said, "We'll be taking about $100 out of the business fund to buy a pack of 10 to get started, I'm sure we'll be putting that $100 back in no time. ...then we'll offer my Uncle Frank free lawn services for access to his equipment and if the cassettes sell like we think they might, when we buy in bulk and save near $50 after taxes, we'll split the savings of the first 10 pack deal we get with my Uncle Roy because of the wear and tear on his equipment ...if the 10 sell fast and we have back-orders, then we can figure out how many more packs we should buy...we're making a $50 net profit every time we sell a pack of tapes at $7 a tape.'

After the conversation, they walked over to The Oasis where Layla was graciously making sales while Niles was on the scene drawing on some paper... some DOPE sketches... When Khalil finally saw the art for the marketing it was, he told Niles about the cassettes and said they would be able to charge more if he could put his art on the cover.

Khalil laid out the plan for Niles because although he posted up with Layla and Rella, helping them a bit he didn't become a partner because of his hot-headed tendencies. He was cool and protective of Layla and Rella, though, so it was the best place for him. Until he mastered composure, he would be hanging out at The Oasis...it was light work, so he was lightly compensated as a 'light associate.'

The cassette tape hustle could possibly give Niles another stream of revenue. With dope artwork, they'd be able to sell exclusive extra-long 90-minute tapes for $10 instead of $7. That definitely changed their profit margin.

Khalil to Niles, 'Ankhal Services won't be accepting partners this summer, but we want to hire you as our resident artist...you can get paid $1 for every cassette you decorate or you can wait till after sales and get $2 for every cassette sold. We will provide your supplies, plus your usual weekly pay for assisting Layla at The Oasis.

...At the moment, he didn't know which was better and admitted as much. Khalil said, "I'll make it easy for you to wait for the sales and get $2 for each instead of $1 upfront for each."

Khalil handed Niles a $10 bill and told him to tuck THE LOAN away and don't let it burn his pockets.

"Nolan and I have your back, and by next summer you should be on the team doing the same as us and better, because you're an artist and will be a partner."

Later that evening, Anton was driving back home from who knows where. He went to find Khalil before going home for the night. Anton told Khalil that Niles might be ready to partner up with them soon after summer is over.

"He's starting to see the value in keeping his cool. That hurt wild animal look in his eyes is not there. I think he sees his value."

Khalil confirmed this by adding,

"Especially since he realizes he could be the reason we charge $3 more dollars a cassette, just because of his artwork."

Anton gave up the 'Ankhal Dap' and then said:

"Remember when he was about to stab that extra heavy double-wide kid that bumped into him by mistake?"

"He's come a long way from that...big chubby dude was in all red, and Niles Crips so hard that he doesn't even drink red Kool-Aid, my cousin came from Cali crazy!"

Anton nodded a laugh, then said:

"In a few weeks we'll test him out to see if he's ready. Tomorrow I have a surprise for you and Nolan, an important surprise."

Later that evening, Khalil, Nolan, and Niles went to Khalil's Uncle Frank's house to record all the latest from Mr. Magic's Rap attack on 107.5 in NY. Niles let the music motivate his art, Khalil and Nolan made sure the music they captured was exclusive.

Chapter Thirteen

SPORTS and SELF DEFENSE

That morning Nolan left Niles in the double-wide where he was doing his drawings. He went to join Anton and Khalil at Sebastian's picnic table.

Anton spoke:

"It's time for me to personally address commandment number nine. You guys have to be responsible with any self-defense lessons you are taught. You guys don't move like bullies, but if you ever do, I'LL FUCK YALL UP!!"

That's the first time they ever heard Anton curse.

Anton then methodically taught them jui-jujitsu. By the time school started again, Khalil was confident in what he could do. He wasn't concerned with running into the younger Watters brothers this upcoming school year. That's probably why it didn't even happen. Bullies couldn't smell any intimidation on Khalil. He had the confidence of a person who could thoroughly defend himself: A MAN.

Anton definitely took fitness seriously and enjoyed watching sports mostly basketball and football. He didn't play any though, he only played chess with life. Khalil took a liking to basketball and began to excel at it. Nolan was the most elusive athlete on any field he was on, with strength and speed to go with his agility.

Anton supported them both as much as he could. During school, the business mostly thrived on the weekends when they were available. During basketball season, Khalil was only rarely available on the weekends, during football season, Nolan was rarely available. They still did okay as a business during the school months, just not nearly as well as in the summer.

Khalil was becoming a very good basketball player ... athletic with great defensive techniques and instincts, offensively, he had an unstoppable midrange game and some effective one-on moves.

Nolan played running back on offense and a safety and defensive back on defense, depending on the package... He belonged on that football field. He always made a difference.

Anton told them that this was the best time to see if they wanted to pursue the sports they liked. This way, when they get to high school, they'll know if they should continue or focus on more on the business. Anton had a sports commandment as well:

Play with passion or don't play at all...

Nolan's response to this commandment:

"I agree, because what's the point of playing it when I

could be helping the business, I'd better be playing it with passion if I'm not doing my part in the business."

Khalil appreciated his response and Anton wondered just how good he could be. Nolan was definitely going to play football in high school, but Khalil was not so sure about himself and basketball.

Khalil really enjoyed the sport, and he thought he could maybe be good enough to get a scholarship. Then he thought that if he kept growing with Anton they'd be able to own a whole league if they wanted. He knew he could always pick up a basketball and go play, but an opportunity to be a successful entrepreneur is here and now. Sebastian always said that timing is everything.

Khalil's decision was made: he wouldn't pursue basketball in high school. However, he strongly felt that Nolan should pursue football and Nolan agreed.

As far as basketball was concerned, it seemed, at least locally, that the trio of Khalil, Nolan, and Niles could not be beaten. They were even beating guys close to Anton's age. Before Sebastian got sick, he put a hoop up on the low-traffic street on the other side of his house for Khalil.

The trio had this unstoppable offensive set they'd run, the pick and roll with Niles on the other side for spacing. Niles was ready to make 15ft wide-open bank shots when his defender was forced to help defend that impossible-to-defend pick and roll that Nolan and Khalil mastered. Khalil rarely had to go into his bag of one-on-one moves...he thought the less he went one-on-one, the more his cousins would be involved and engaged.

Chapter Fourteen

THE ESSENCE OF ADOLESCENCE

Summer business was going well. So well that the weather forecast was no problem. It was looked at as a day off, and that was a rarity in the summer. The forecast was rain, and the only days they took off were in the summertime except Sundays. Those loud thunderstorms that rocked the southeast in the summer starred in the day's weather...on and off, all day. As part-time farmers under Anton's tutelage, the cousins always paid attention to the weather forecast. They put a tarp over everything they needed to, The Oasis and their carts mainly.

It was a day basically to lounge in the nice-sized attic Sebastian prepared for Khalil. They listened to Nolan's boom box, played gin rummy, and talked about girls.

"Remember what Anton told us about them," Khalil continued, "Don't be afraid to approach the most attractive woman in the room, but until then, keep handling your business and your attraction will increase."

"Yeah, the only commandment he gave us about women," Nolan was mocking and continued, "I just want to be good with all that kissing, licking, and stroking. I could've got some already, but I got nervous and I went soft. Fast ass Yolanda still be giggling about that."

Khalil and Niles always joked that Nolan was going to be out here getting these women pregnant left and right. Nolan was the oldest, and he'd be the first of them to enter high school. At the time, Nolan was in the 8th grade, Khalil was a 7th grader, and Niles was in the 6th. They all had girlfriends, but nothing heavy was happening, the only one who was really anxious to have sex was Nolan.

Khalil noticed how many attractive girls were available and felt no need to rush it. The really attractive ones didn't pay him any attention anyway. Not the ones he was drawn to.

Khalil wanted to understand himself better before entering a girl. Meanwhile, Niles has already gotten 'mean top' from an older girl, a 16-year-old named Belinda.

She was visiting from Florida for the summer and always came around them. She started liking Khalil at first because Anton didn't even count. However, Khalil's girlfriend at the time was her younger cousin she was visiting, so she soon went for Niles. Ironically she ignored Nolan, the oldest and horniest one of the three.

It was something about Nile's' Cali swag, and Belinda just wanted someone to practice 'going down' on because she was looking forward to doing that well for her true crush back in Florida. Niles was waiting like Khalil, but he still liked to play with himself to simulate that great 'head action' Belinda turned him on to.

After experiencing Belinda's services 3 times in 2 days, Niles told Khalil with a devilish grin, that he needed to let Belinda teach her cousin (Khalil's girlfriend) some things. Then told Nolan and Khalil how great fellatio is to receive.

Nolan responded:

"You better learn how to give it to...get with her and practice that."

Then Nolan put his baseball cap on and informed them he was about to lose his virginity that evening.

"Me and Reesha doing it tonight... she knows Rochelle likes me, and how much she wants to give me some...now Reesha is ready to act right."

Khalil spoke up:

'Why don't you just kindly break up with Reesha, then do it too fast ass Rochelle, since she's already ready.'

Khalil didn't want Reesha to get hurt; she was a class-mate, and they had been cool since elementary school.

"Cuz, I've been wanting Reesha too long to play it like that."

Then Nolan walked out the door. Khalil shrugged his shoulders, and thought, it ain't like she doesn't have a choice.

Chapter Fifteen

ANTON

As a teenager, Anton was a dream to the ladies, it was basically unfair. A fly money-making junior in high school, he was adored by the girls and envied by the guys.

Anton was 6'0 even and had the look of those dark Dominicans, Panamanians, or even Trinidadians. He was of medium build and his workouts had him ripped at 180 pounds. He was topped off with that naturally soft, dark, curly hair. Layla and Monifah had big crushes on Anton. Even Khalil's sophisticated cousin Cynthia would swoon for him, but Anton would never.

Besides being far too young, he knew full well it would be bad for business anyway. He didn't even pay attention to high school girls. He actually preferred 18 and up.

He lost his virginity to a sexy older (about 35) beauty shop owner named Henrietta a year earlier. He met her when he went into her establishment, passing out business cards advertising Ankhal's Services food carts and The Oasis stand. She hired Ankhal Services to maintain her landscaping, and sometimes, they'd run errands for her, which included mostly deliveries from their Garlington Heights food truck. Her shop was in that area.

She playfully flirted with Anton in what seemed like a contest, trying to get him to blush. He wasn't shy, though, and more direct than most men. This made her blush instead. He honestly told her he was a virgin, but he understands what to do and is looking forward to the thrill. After that, he only had to convince her that he took full responsibility and it was their secret.

Anton was having relations with her for about 3 months. She thought this young 15-year-old was the most real 'man' in Waycross. When she realized she revered him, she left him alone. She knew she'd be asking for trouble if she let herself get totally whipped by a 15-year-old boy. He was certainly different, and extraordinarily mature, but still.

She had a reality check and actually laughed at herself, wondering what would happen if she got pregnant by young Anton. Henrietta wistfully moved on. Two months later, soon after she took her age group seriously again and got involved with a local electrician. It wasn't anything surreal, but it worked for a while.

They never got married or had kids. They did shack up for about a year before he went back to his family (with a woman who had two of his kids, but he never married) on the other side of town. Henrietta would be damned before she had his baby. They could have their fun, though from time to time.

Chapter Sixteen

The Jerri curl was the slick, greasy look the 80s offered. By this time, the 'black' community was programmed to despise their natural hair. Anton thought it was a goofy fad, so of course, Khalil was totally against it.

Anton didn't need one. However, Khalil took the time to learn about his own course hair. He found out that he just had to keep his hair moisturized and then lock in the moisture with some quality oils. It was that simple. All the cousins agreed that every Saturday, they would be ritually at the barbershop to maintain their varied styles. Khalil's Afro, Nolan's Caesar, and Niles' bald fade topped with waves.

Arrangements were made for Monifah to stay with her grandparents. After her grandfather (Ellis) accessed the situation, he figured it would be a good idea if Monifah lived with them. She would be a great help around the house, and she'll be able to join her cousin Layla at The Oasis.

Khalil was happy his sister would not have to deal with that cult (JW's). He would make sure his older sister was straight. Whatever she wanted to do, he would help her do it.

The only requirement from their mother was they would have to spend most of the summer of '86 with her. She now resides in NJ (Willingboro). About 20 minutes from Philadelphia.

THE CRUNK TAPES WERE ALL THE RAGE IN Waycross. The barbershops had them in stock, as well as certain convenience stores. Of course, Henrietta's beauty shop had those Crunk Tapes available. By this time, they were up to Volume 4. Mr. Magic (107.5 kWBLS) gave them these artists in 1985:

RUN DMC, Fat Boys, Kurtis Blow, LL Cool J, Too Short, Boogie Boys, Mantronix, Schooly D, UTFO, Roxanne Shante, Beastie Boys, Steady B, Force MD's, Craig G and a few more.

That first 10-pack sold in less than an hour...after that day, the streets were buzzing. They didn't want a hand-me-down carbon copy of the original Crunk Tapes; they wanted that original sound from the master tape. Full bass was loud and the highs crisp, with no hissing. The artwork component was a trendsetter. Niles's artwork really set the purchase of a Crunk Tape apart.

Regardless, at the end of the day, the engine of their foray into selling cassettes was that exclusive hip-hop music.

The same day, they immediately went back to buy 10-10 packs of cassettes for $150, then went to work making high-quality copies from the master tapes...Niles' artwork was requested elsewhere, so he freelanced a bit.

Niles even repainted the immobilized truck, SEBASTIAN'S ROASTED PEANUTS (he'd always hear of the behind-the-scenes exploits of Sebastian. Anton, Nolan, and Khalil would talk about how much of a gem Sebastian was. How instrumental Sebastian was to the business, warm words of love and respect for their 'silent' partner). So, like only Niles could, he made 1019 Blackwell Street a definitive landmark. Especially after he redid The Oasis sign pro bono just to bring more advertising to himself.

All this good work and early success, yet an official partner in Ankhal Services, is what Niles wanted. Truth is, though, Niles was a very dangerous, scared kid at this point in his life.

As long as he could run, and he wasn't cornered, he wasn't a threat. However, if cornered, he had an ice pick type of weapon that would prove very harmful to whoever tried to corner and bully him courtesy of watching his Uncle Khalan create makeshift weapons.

One of the reasons Anton wasn't anxious to make Niles a partner in the business was because of the strange vibes Niles gave off. Something seemed off, and Anton wanted time to reveal what may be the issue with Niles.

One day, Niles rode his bike to the store for firecrackers, another cap gun, particular drawing pens and pencils for the cassette tape artwork and other drawings he did. That's when he had the unfortunate interaction with Lamarcus and Orion Watters.

They saw him going into the store and they decided to have some fun bullying him. Since they knew Niles would most likely be purchasing firecrackers, they would take them too. Everyone knows Niles loves firecrackers. Fireworks period.

The Oasis basically had all the refreshments he needed for a hot day, so the younger Watters' bullies were sure he was buying a cap gun or some type of toy, not snacks.

As Niles was coming out of the store, he didn't notice the Watters right away. They caught him slipping and pounced on him as soon as he finished unlocking his bike (they planned to take that, too). Lamarcus bullied with glee, so with a smile on his face, he grabbed Niles from behind and threw him to the ground. The younger, Orion, was more sinister in disposition, kicked Niles in his side with all his athletic might after Lamarcus slammed him down, then Orion took his store purchases that were in a bag lying on the ground.

Lamarcus started to go for the bike. He was tired of Orion riding on his handlebars these past days. Orion had lost his bike trying to jump over a deep creek. The current carried the bike too far to worry about it anymore, plus Orion had to get himself to safety.

Fortunately for Niles, Anton happened to be breezing by, riding his bike for a change of pace, when he noticed the commotion.

He noticed Niles in pain on the ground and charges to the rescue. As soon as the Watters brothers saw Anton, they ran, Lamarcus didn't even get to take the bike, but they did get his bag of supplies and toys.

After helping Niles get himself together, he asked Niles

about the sharp object that he saw him pull out as he was approaching to help. Niles was enraged and couldn't express himself because of it. His body was still shaking a bit. After Niles was finally able to relax, he showed Anton his makeshift weapon. Niles said he'd only use it for anyone trying to gang up on him or sneak up on him because he can fight like his dad. He added that his dad never lost...EVER!!

Anton was glad that he happened to be going that way because if Niles had got the opportunity, he could've got some dangerous jabs in with that weapon, and it would've really been a bad situation. He took the weapon from Niles and then went back into the store with Niles to replace his art supplies. He told Niles that his supplies should be an expense covered by the business anyway since it's for the business. Anton paid for his other drawing supplies, too, on that occasion. Niles had some clientele for his art; he was that good.

Later that evening a simple situation ended very violently as Payne's jealousy and animosity of Anton reared its ugly head.

As Anton was entering the convenience store to play his grandparent's numbers, he heard Payne and his crew talking loudly about nothing, passing around a bottle of something strong, getting wasted. One member was too 'sauced up,' and after Anton entered the store, Shannon spat out his words drunkenly,

"Ain't that the lil business dude that gave you a lesson!"

As soon as Shannon said those words, he felt fear and remorse. It struck him immediately after he said it that he shouldn't have said a damn thing. The ridiculous power of alcohol.

Before commencing to severely injure Shannon, Payne responded loudly and angrily,

"NIGGA I WAS 12 WHEN THAT HAPPENED 5 YEARS AGO!!"

Then he mellowed as he added...

"We all grown now."

As Payne stood at 6'5, 235 mostly muscle mass, he smoothly added,

"Your ass-whipping is going to be the best and the worst lesson. you figure out which."

Payne then smiled at him before faking to hand him the bottle, Shannon reached as expected and lethargically so because he was already very drunk. Payne punished his cheek with the bottle, smashing it brutally against his face, then came up with an uppercut to the jaw that made the whole crew moan, laid Shannon out. Payne then stomped on his chest with a menacing glare before leaving with the rest of the crew (now just 3 deep in his '75 rusty Chrysler Cordoba).

Payne felt pure larceny for Anton; he never learned from nor got his lesson for trying to bully.

Meanwhile, Anton never thought about Payne too much at all...that was until he saw one of Payne's longest-tenured buddies all bloody and struggling to get up. Anton went and got some material out of the trunk of the Pinto, then covered up the passenger seat. After that was done, he helped Shannon to the car, dropped him off at the emergency room, and then contacted his parents. Shannon's diagnosis was a broken jaw, lacerations to the face, and a chest contusion.

After those ordeals with the Watters, Anton decided he

wanted to expand his knowledge of the arts. He was well-versed in jui-jujitsu, but he wanted to be effective with his hands. Fortunately, he was able to get a tutorial VHS of Sugar Ray Leonard and Tommy Hearns teaching the basics of boxing.

Every first Saturday of the month, they had a business meeting. At the next meeting, Anton would suggest getting boxing equipment so they could all learn the art of hitting without getting hit.

Niles wouldn't be taught any jui-jujitsu form of defense until he officially became a partner in Ankhal Services, but being nice with his hands like his dad should certainly be cultivated. That's how Anton saw it.

When it came to boxing, Khalil stayed on the fringes of it... not wanting to get hit ever was his thing, so he entertained boxing enough to get the gist of how to defend and counter. Khalil was more into diffusing fights.

As with most things, Nolan excelled at boxing too. His reflexes and movement were all but forgotten after you saw his blazing speed and otherworldly power. The problem with Nolan was the same as Khalil's: not EVER wanting to get hit. The difference, though, was if you forced Nolan to defend himself against you, he was prone to be more spiteful towards you than Khalil.

Nolan had more range in comparison to Khalil. He could be far crueler than Khalil, but he could also be far more compassionate as well.

Chapter Seventeen

NILES IS READY

It just turned August (still 1985), less than another month of a very productive summer for Ankhal Services. Anton gathered the trio together to discuss Niles's partnership with Ankhal Services.

It was Sunday, and they all met up in front of The Oasis. Anton, Nolan, Khalil, and Niles waited for Chris to pull up in one of their business vehicles. The '72 F250 camper truck. Chris loved maneuvering that vehicle.

He pulled up, and they all got in. They were headed to The Huddle House for breakfast and business. They had a light conversation about the neighborhood and joked about a few crazy moments that happened over the summer. The next thing you knew, their breakfast platters were ready. They ate heartily after Chris said grace. Anton then directed everyone's attention to Ankhal's Business commandments.

Anton decided to read each commandment and then let Chris, Nolan, and Khalil decide if Niles had the qualities to honor each one.

Since, at this point, they all had confidence in Niles, it all seemed like a formality more than anything else. Niles became an official partner of Ankhal Services in the restaurant that a.m.

Chris then decided to bring up Shannon.

"Shannon is all healed up from Payne's hotheaded beat down. He wants to be a part of what we're doing. He said he doesn't drink anymore and is back in school doing the right thing. He said the only thing that will prevent him from shooting Payne is if he could get successful with us."

Chris added:

"I remember when he was younger, he was a good kid until Payne corrupted him. He was basically a scared follower, with the alcohol providing fake courage. He just needs a better example to follow. I'll talk to him and feel him out a bit to be sure."

Anton responded:

"We can't take any risks with Shannon...I can get him a job at Hardce's, I'm cool with a manager there, if he can keep that job for a while, then we can consider it."

Khalil then gave Niles the 'Ankhal Dap' as a ritual to welcome him to the group, then everyone else followed suit. Niles was elated, then added,

"You're real careful about who gets in, that's why I'm so geeked, I know I belong because I see that y'all believe in me. More importantly, I'm starting to believe in my damn self!!!'

Anton responded,

"To protect the reputation of our business, my number

one job is to be very careful about partnerships with Ankhal Services."

EARLIER THAT SAME MORNING...

The package came, two huge boxes mailed to 1019 Blackwell Street.

"What's in those boxes?"

Niles asked this earlier as Chris was pulling up. Anton said he was looking forward to showing them after a good breakfast. He then asked the curious Niles to put the boxes in the bed of the truck after Chris pulled up, of course Khalil and Nolan helped. It was a natural thing, they always helped each other, it was a reflex that helped to bond them.

FAST FORWARD...

Now walking out of The Huddle House, approaching the truck to go back home, Anton went to the boxes and unveiled their shirts in the first box they opened. Shirts for everyone involved in Ankhal Services. Seven shirts each. Niles joined just in time, he thought. They also had shirts for Layla and Monifah to bring to them.

"We're rocking that Crip blue," he thought to himself.

The other box contained jackets for the guys with the business logo. They were going to look very professional moving forward.

It was a laidback day for the guys, just relaxing around The Oasis all day while Monifah and Layla managed the stand as usual. Nolan mentioned to Niles that he could teach him some Jiu-Jitsu now that he's a partner. Niles just smiled.

Later in the early evening, the trio spent another Sunday dominating the local competition as usual, playing 3 on 3.

Meanwhile, Anton went off to who knows where, and Chris went to Savannah to visit an old crush from high school. She was going to college there.

Chapter Eighteen

This summer would be different. Anton was to graduate high school. Khalil and Monifah were to spend 2 months of summer in NJ with their mom, stepdad and younger brother.

The only requirement their mom had that Khalil winced at was going to the Kingdom Hall every Sunday a.m. Cutting the grass and other yard work was fine with Khalil. Monifah showed her worth inside the home, keeping things tidy, and showing off her cooking skills courtesy of mastering those dishes she helped prepare for The Oasis food carts. Monifah stayed in the house most of the time, reading. Occasionally, though, Khalil would get her to ride the bike trail with him to get her some fresh air.

Khalil usually spent most of his time at the basketball court at Hawthorne Elementary School. He quickly made a friend there; his name was Louis. After a few days of clowning Khalil's country accent, Louis left the jokes alone and seriously considered what Khalil was telling him about Ankhal Services back home. Louis was impressed when Khalil showed him a business card. Louis asked for one so he could show his stepdad.

Khalil knew Louis would fit in well as a partner with Ankhal Services. All Khalil and Louis did was talk about business ideas, girls, and basketball. Louis was girl crazy but could play it off so well that it was hard to tell. It mostly seemed like girls couldn't get enough of him, the truth was in the middle.

Louis told him about his summer job helping his stepdad detail vehicles in Philly. He didn't like how dirty his hands and nails got. He did like that money, though.

Louis finessed the management at the local Domino's Pizza into letting them pass out flyers for pay pizza (an idea that enhanced business nicely). Twice a week, they did this for Dominoes and for their efforts, they were rewarded $20 each and an XL free pizza to take home to their respective families two times a week.

Khalil's interaction with Louis gave him more business ideas to incorporate into Ankhal Services. A pressure washer for car washing and detailing, plus ways to advertise services better.

He also learned some tactics when it came to the girls. Louis was smooth, and some of that rubbed off on Khalil. Some of that 'New Jersey swagger.'

Khalil made a couple of mixtapes from a Princeton channel. They played amazing 'unheard of' 'underground' rappers, but the quality of the sound wasn't optimal because of the reception. He just kept that for his personal archives. Khalil was able to get some high-quality mixes from 'Street Beat' Lady B (WUSL Power 98.9FM), a Philly station.

Khalil enjoyed his visit to NJ overall, he just didn't appreciate those Sunday mornings (mournings) at the Kingdom Hall.

Their mother was a devout Jehovah's Witness and stayed the course. Khalil was not and stayed his course. His mother realized this, so that would be the last summer he visited their mother. She did not want her youngest son 'corrupted' by Khalil, nor the child she was carrying. Khalil would have a half-brother soon.

Khalil promised Louis that when his older cousin Nolan got his license, they would take the 95 S road trip north to visit again. Khalil meant to keep his word on that, even though that was two summers away.

The end of June was quickly approaching, and Khalil was looking forward to the month of July in Willingboro, but he had to leave immediately, something about Anton.

Time to go back to Waycross, to family and business. Monifah stayed while Khalil took a flight to Jacksonville Airport where his Uncle Chris was waiting.

Chapter Nineteen

THE SUMMER OF '86 BACK HOME

WHILE KHALIL WAS GONE, ANTON AND NILES combined to handle 80% of his responsibilities, the other 20% was absorbed by Chris and Nolan. Layla was challenged a bit at first with the absence of Monifah, but Uncle Roy's youngest daughter (also Chris' niece) proved to be very helpful in just a week after learning the ropes. Retta was a great addition to Ankhal Services.

Chris had a heart-to-heart with Shannon, and Shannon admitted that he needed help with alcohol addiction.

Chris spoke with Anton, and they decided to get him help at a facility for rehabilitation. They decided to try the Treatment Center of Waycross.

"If Shannon could truly rehabilitate himself and he agrees to Ankhal Business Commandments, he's in. He just has to put some work in at Hardee's, at least a year. We can't take alcoholism lightly. The business could suffer if we brought him on and he goes in remission."

Anton was adamant about this.

At this point Anton was a 17-year-old approaching graduation. He earned good grades throughout just out of respect to the ones that paved the way for him.

His own grandfather, of course Sebastian-Khalil's grandfather, and Khalil's other grandad Ellis, the one Khalil shares with Nolan and Niles. Anton understood why Nolan felt the way he did about school.

"Ankhal Services was 'schoolin' us!" Anton would always say this after something challenging happened during the business day. Regardless of understanding Nolan's point, he'd never promote giving subpar effort in anything assigned to a person. Handle your responsibilities with pride was his mantra.

Before Khalil left, Anton had a talk with him about things going forward upon his return.

"Khalil, you and Chris have to pick up my slack when I get ready to leave for the Army. We won't depend on it, but if Shannon is rehabilitated, we'll have another partner."

Khalil didn't want Anton to leave for the military.

"Why are you even going into the military, and when did you say you're leaving for basic training?"

'I'll be getting Ankhal Services worldwide connections like Mr. Nelson. I leave the week after Labor Day to Ft. Knox. That gives us plenty of time to make all the necessary transitions when you get back from up north in August. Be safe up there in NJ, lil bro."

"It's some suburbs, I should be fine."

Anton wanted to see what was abroad and gain new

experiences, so he signed up. Anton kept his discussion brief with Khalil, with no filler, straight to the point, then off on one of his 'missions.'

Anton's been off doing his own thing more than ever lately, basically just getting his affairs in order. He also started creeping around with Henrietta again with much more frequency. Their secret rendezvous added to the excitement.

One time, she told him to feel her without the condom for a moment, then putting the condom on felt so good he never put the condom on; in that episode, he spilled his seed deep in her. Afterwards, he thought about the scenario and shrugged. That time, she didn't get pregnant.

Although Anton had a town full of options, he had a very low body count. Besides Henrietta, only two other women could honestly say Anton was with them intimately.

Those two young women were away at different colleges in the state now, women who would soon be college graduates. It'd always been older women for Anton. He always wanted to be around people he may learn something from, and that included his sex partners.

Right after he graduated high school at seventeen years old, Anton impregnated Henrietta in what happened to be their most intensely satisfying session. He became addicted to the 'raw feeling' combined with the fact that she was so pleasantly pleased and spent from multiple orgasms that she dared not move. She didn't take her usual precautions. This is the reason why she takes accountability anyway.

She was almost 39, about to have her first child... the electrician thought it was his because they still dabbled with each other for different reasons. Her affair with Anton was very private and quiet except for a few hushed gossip sessions by her beauticians, who could sense the spark between them. Whenever he had to deliver platters or receive payments for the landscaping, you could see the spark between them.

It was the beginning of July, a month after Anton's graduation, about two months before his basic training date on a late Saturday evening. He was returning home from a Hotel rendezvous with Henrietta just outside of town.

Payne Watters and Derrick Blackhead were drunk driving in dark moods. They must've been drinking that brown (cognac)... It was rumored that Payne dared the younger Derrick to run the stop sign to sideswipe Anton on his favorite toy. They planned to just to scare him and scuff his Kawasaki Ninja (a gift from his grandfather Quinn).

Payne was so jealous of Anton and bitter from the old scenario. The way Anton made him pay for trying to bully him. Derrick Blackhead was an incorrigible knucklehead. The one who stole Khalil's bike that time way back. Now 15 with no license, Derrick was doing the most. (Unlicensed and underage drinking. A horrible combination).

Derrick could've sworn he only grazed Anton's motorcycle, but the impact seemed more than what it should've been, he thought. When Derrick looked over at Payne, he knew something was wrong. Payne was looking out his side of the window in utter shock. They went too far. Anton's bike was totaled. Anton was facedown and motionless. These circumstances sobered the duo quickly as they realized their ridiculousness.

They didn't turn themselves in. They ran and lived in

the woods for about 48 hours before they were discovered and arrested. It had to be the longest two days of miserable and paranoid freedom. Not only did the slight dent and paint exchange confirm they did it, but there was an eyewitness, two in fact. It was a speedy trial, and Waycross didn't seem the same after this horrible incident.

That vehicular incident killed Anton. Seventeen years old. Derrick went to prison for vehicular homicide, maxed out at 10 years. Since Payne was the older person in charge, plus the vehicle was in his name, he received a sentence as well, only 5 years in his case.

It would prove to be one of the saddest days in Khalil's life when he got back from NJ 2 days after it happened. Anton proved to be the best influence he could've asked for, a Godsend.

After all the mourning and proceedings, what stood out to Khalil was Quinn's last words of his eulogy:

"I always told him to enjoy his childhood, thinking it would be the shortest period of his life but I was wrong. The young man only had a short time to be with us, but he had a lot he wanted to accomplish. I'm so proud of my grandson. REST IN PEACE DEAR BOY.

I certainly shouldn't be burying my grandson, it's not the natural way."

Some tears finally decided to trickle down the side of his face as he left the podium. He seemed a bit defeated, he buried his son, and now his grandson.

NOLAN WAS 14 NOW, AND KHALIL WOULD BE LATER in the year. Niles was 13. They had some serious shoes to fill. Because Anton was planning to do a stint in the military, they never got a food truck. The business must be run by the trio now...with solid help from Chris and Vance.

Back lounging in the attic, attempting to get out of a somber mood, Khalil brought up Anton's commandment about girls:

"Never be afraid to approach the most attractive girl in the room. It's the equivalent of saying go for what you want and don't settle."

Khalil acknowledged his feelings sexually:

"I think I'm ready for the pleasure of sex, but if I'm honest with myself, I have to ask, am I ready for the responsibility that having sex brings."

Niles said, "Cuz I'm 'bout ready, catch up!" They all laughed.

Then Khalil got serious, "When we do whatever we're about to do, especially if it's questionable, we've got to ask ourselves, what would Anton do?"

They said the good die young; Khalil believed it as it concerned Anton.

MEANWHILE, NOLAN WAS DISTRACTED BY thoughts of Reesha. It felt so exquisite inside her, tight and wet. The proper pressure made him lose control fast. He didn't use a condom and surely exploded powerfully inside her. She complained harshly about Nolan's orgasm filling her up. She was scared of the great possibility of being pregnant. She enjoyed the foreplay, but the actual sex seemed like a chore or initiation of some sort. She did not want to be pregnant at 13, but the peer pressure of Nolan was too much. He just had to have it. The best things in life for Nolan were his cousins (Khalil and Niles), football, and sex.

HOW DO THEY MOVE FORWARD WITHOUT ANTON? ...stay tuned and find out.